This book was purchased for the
Nowata City/County Library
by
The Kathleen & W.W. Warner Fund

Thanksgiving

Sandy Sepehri

FITZGERALD BOOKS

Bethany, Missouri

Photo Credits:
Cover © Library of Congress; Title Page, Pages 5, 22 © Sean Locke; Pages 6, 7, 9, 10, 11, 15, 17 © Library of
Congress; Page 13 © Michael West; Page 19 © PIR, Lisa F. Young; Page 21 © Lisa F. Young

Cataloging-in-Publication Data

Sepehri, Sandy
    Thanksgiving / Sandy Sepehri. — 1st ed.
    p. cm. — (American holidays)

    Includes bibliographical references and index.
    Summary: Text and photographs introduce the history of
Thanksgiving Day, including when, how, and why it is celebrated.
    ISBN-13: 978-1-4242-1345-0 (lib. bdg. : alk. paper)
    ISBN-10: 1-4242-1345-2 (lib. bdg. : alk. paper)
    ISBN-13: 978-1-4242-1435-8 (pbk. : alk. paper)
    ISBN-10: 1-4242-1435-1 (pbk. : alk. paper)

    1. Pilgrims (New Plymouth Colony)—Juvenile literature.
2. Thanksgiving Day—Juvenile literature.
3. United States—Social life and customs—Juvenile literature.
[1. Pilgrims (New Plymouth Colony).
2. Massachusetts—History—New Plymouth, 1620-1691.
3. Thanksgiving Day. 4. Wampanoag Indians—History.
5. Holidays. 6. United States—Social life and customs.] I. Sepehri, Sandy. II. Title. III. Series.
    F68.S47 2007
    974.4'8202—dc22

First edition
© 2007 Fitzgerald Books
802 N. 41st Street, P.O. Box 505
Bethany, MO 64424, U.S.A.
Printed in China
Library of Congress Control Number: 2006941005

Table of Contents

What Is Thanksgiving?

Thanksgiving is an American holiday. It is always the fourth Thursday of November.

On Thanksgiving we gather with family and friends to enjoy food and each other's company. This is also a special time to be grateful for the good things in our lives.

Thanksgiving is a tradition that was started long ago by the **Pilgrims**. The Pilgrims sailed to America from Europe in 1620, on a ship named the *Mayflower*.

They came to a place they named New Plymouth, which is in what we now call the state of Massachusetts.

They wanted to have more room for their homes and their **crops**. They also wanted freedom to follow their own **religion**.

The Pilgrims and the Wampanoag

In the new land, the Pilgrims had trouble growing food. They found help from a group of Native-American tribes, called the Wampanoag Nation.

The Wampanoag people taught the Pilgrims how to plant corn and other crops. They also showed them how to hunt wild turkeys.

13

One of the Wampanoag people knew English. His name was Squanto. He taught the pilgrims to plant fish with the corn seed, which helped the corn grow.

15

The First Thanksgiving Feast

The next year, in 1621, they held a **feast** to give special thanks to God for their new homes, their new friends, and their **harvest** of food.

They invited the Wampanoag people to join them.

The feast included turkey, fish, and corn. The Wampanoag brought deer meat. There may have been cranberries and pumpkin, too.

Pumpkin

Pumpkin Pie

The feast lasted for three days, with eating, dancing, and games. Today we still celebrate Thanksgiving by having fun together.

It is a day to be thankful for the people who love you and for the food you are given.

Glossary

crops (KROPS) — a collection of plants that have been grown for food

feast (FEEST) — a large fancy meal, meant for a gathering of people

harvest (HAR vist) — the collected crops, used for food

Pilgrims (PIL grims) — the people who left Europe in the 1620s to sail to America

religion (ree LIJ en) — an organized system of worshipping God

Index

FURTHER READING

Gibbons, Gail. *Thanksgiving Is....* Holiday House, 2004.
Goode, Diane. *Thanksgiving Is Here!* HarperCollins, 2003.
Ziefert, Harriet. *This Is Thanksgiving.* Blue Apple Books, 2004.

WEBSITES TO VISIT

Because Internet links change so often, Fitzgerald Books has developed an online list of websites related to the subject of this book. This site is updated regularly. Please use this link to access the list: www.fitzgeraldbookslinks.com/ah/tha

ABOUT THE AUTHOR

Sandy Sepehri is an honors graduate from the University of Central Florida. She has authored several children's books and is a columnist for a parents' magazine.